Here Comes PETER COTTONTAIL!

Written by Steve Nelson and Jack Rollins

Song illustrated by Pamela R. Levy

Stickers and fold-out pages
illustrated by Lisa S. Reed

ideals children's books.

Nashville, Tennessee

ISBN-13: 978-0-8249-5639-4

Published by Ideals Children's Books
An imprint of Ideals Publications
A Guideposts Company
Nashville, Tennessee
www.idealsbooks.com

Designed by Georgina Chidlow-Rucker

Color separations by Precision Color Graphics, Franklin, Wisconsin
Printed and bound in China

Leo_Nov12_1

Here comes Peter Cottontail,
Hoppin' down the bunny trail,

Hippity-hoppin', Easter's on its way.
Bringin' every girl and boy

Baskets full of Easter joy,
Things to make your Easter bright and gay.

He's got jellybeans for Tommy,

Colored eggs for sister Sue.

There's an orchid for your mommy

And an Easter bonnet too.

Oh! Here comes
Peter Cottontail,

Hoppin' down the bunny trail,
Hippity-hoppity, happy Easter Day.

Here comes Peter Cottontail,

Hoppin' down the bunny trail,

Look at him stop, and listen to him say,

"Try to do the things you should."

Maybe if you're extra good,

He'll roll lots of Easter eggs your way.

You'll wake up on Easter morning

And you'll know that he was there

When you find those choc'late bunnies

That he's hiding ev'rywhere.

Oh! Here comes Peter Cottontail,
Hoppin' down the bunny trail,

Hippity-hoppity,

Happy Easter Day!